WE'RE MAKING BREAKFAST FOR MOTHER

by **Shirley Neitzel**

pictures by
Nancy Winslow Parker

Greenwillow Books, New York

For my mother,
Ida Wegner Koehler,
who never had breakfast
in bed
—S. N.

For Beechie,
who did have breakfast
in bed
—N. W. P.

Watercolor paints, colored pencils,
and a black pen were used for
the full-color art.
The text type is Seagull Light.

Text copyright © 1997 Shirley Neitzel
Illustrations copyright © 1997
by Nancy Winslow Parker

Printed in Singapore by Tien Wah Press
First Edition
10 9 8 7 6 5 4 3 2 1

Library of Congress
Cataloging-in-Publication Data

Neitzel, Shirley.
We're making breakfast for mother /
by Shirley Neitzel ;
pictures by Nancy Winslow Parker.
        p.   cm.
Summary: Rhymes and rebuses
show children making breakfast for
their mother, complete with flowers
and a tray.
ISBN 0-688-14575-2 (trade)
ISBN 0-688-14576-0 (lib. bdg.)
[1. Breakfasts—Fiction.
2. Stories in rhyme   3. Rebuses.]
I. Parker, Nancy Winslow, ill.   II. Title.
PZ8.3.N34We   1997   [Fic]—dc20
96-10417   CIP   AC

We're making breakfast for Mother.

We know she'll have a super day,

since we're making breakfast for Mother.

We're fixing up this shiny tray.

We know she'll have a super day,
since we're making breakfast for Mother.

Here are some flowers
(we picked her a bunch)

that decorate this shiny

We know she'll have a super day,
since we're making breakfast for Mother.

Here is the cereal, the kind that goes crunch,

that's next to the (we picked her a bunch)

that decorate this shiny

We know she'll have a super day,
since we're making breakfast for Mother.

Here is the sugar, lumpy and sweet,

that's for the the kind that goes crunch,

that's next to the (we picked her a bunch)

that decorate this shiny

We know she'll have a super day,
since we're making breakfast for Mother.

Here is the tea (we brewed her a pot)

for dunking the (we made whole wheat).

It's beside the lumpy and sweet,

that's for the the kind that goes crunch,

that's next to the 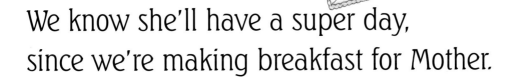 (we picked her a bunch)

that decorate this shiny

We know she'll have a super day,
since we're making breakfast for Mother.

Here's a banana, with only one spot,

we put by the 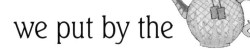 (we brewed her a pot)

for dunking the (we made whole wheat).

It's beside the lumpy and sweet,

that's for the the kind that goes crunch,

that's next to the  (we picked her a bunch)

that decorate this shiny

We know she'll have a super day,
since we're making breakfast for Mother.

Here is the jelly, sticky and bright,

that's near the 🍌 with only one spot,

we put by the 🫖 (we brewed her a pot)

for dunking the 🍞 (we made whole wheat).

It's beside the 🍯 lumpy and sweet,

that's for the 🥣 the kind that goes crunch,

that's next to the 💐 (we picked her a bunch)

that decorate this shiny 🍽️ BGM

We know she'll have a super day,
since we're making breakfast for Mother.

Here is some milk, frosty and white,

to stand by the 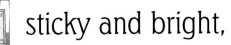 sticky and bright,

that's near the with only one spot,

we put by the (we brewed her a pot)

for dunking the (we made whole wheat).

It's beside the lumpy and sweet,

that's for the  the kind that goes crunch,

that's next to the 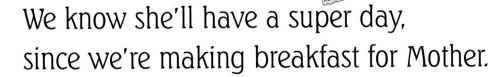 (we picked her a bunch)

that decorate this shiny

We know she'll have a super day,
since we're making breakfast for Mother.

"Good morning, Mother. Happy day!
Look at the flowers
we've picked for your tray.

"Here's some milk. It was hard to pour.
We brought you cereal.
Some spilled on the floor.

"Here's sugar and tea—it's not very hot—
and a banana with only one spot.

"Here's whole wheat toast,
 a little too brown,
 with raspberry jelly . . .
 Oops! Jelly-side down!"

"You made me breakfast? I'm impressed!

"Let's share this feast and then get dressed.

"We'll put on our jackets and go for a hike,

since I don't want to see
what the kitchen looks like."

"It's fun making breakfast for Mother!"